It's Quacking Time!

For John Joseph Harrison,
weight 7 lb. 11 oz. ·∾· M. W.

For Harry James Humphreys,
my grandson ·∾· J. B.

Text copyright © 2005 by Martin Waddell
Illustrations copyright © 2005 by Jill Barton

First U.S. edition 2005

Library of Congress Cataloging-in-Publication Data is available.

Library of Congress Cataloging Card Number pending.

ISBN 0-7636-2738-0

10 9 8 7 6 5 4 3 2 1

Printed in Singapore

This book was typeset in Esprit Medium.
The illustrations were done in watercolor and pencil.

Candlewick Press
2067 Massachusetts Avenue
Cambridge, Massachusetts 02140

visit us at www.candlewick.com

It's Quacking Time!

Martin Waddell

illustrated by **Jill Barton**

CANDLEWICK PRESS
CAMBRIDGE, MASSACHUSETTS

Duckling lived in the rushes
with Mommy and Daddy.

One day Mommy Duck laid an egg.

It was pale blue.

Mommy and Daddy were excited, but . . .

Duckling had never seen a duck egg before.

"What's that thing?" asked Duckling.

"It's our egg," Mommy said.

"Our egg, with a baby duck in it."

"Did I come in one of those eggs?"
Duckling asked Daddy.

"You did," Daddy said.
"Your egg was lovely!"

Auntie Duck came up from her nest in the reeds.

"Mommy laid our egg," Duckling told Auntie.

"It's our egg, with a baby duck in it. I came
in one too. Daddy says my egg was lovely."

"I remember your egg," Auntie said.

"How did I fit in my egg?" Duckling asked Auntie.

"You were much smaller then," Auntie said.

"You had to be small to fit in the egg."

Grandpa Duck swam up from the end of the lake.

"That's our egg, with a baby duck in it," Duckling

told Grandpa. "I came in one too. Auntie says

I had to be small to fit in my egg . . . but I don't

remember my egg."

"I don't remember mine either," said Grandpa.

"Did you come in an egg?" Duckling gasped.

"All ducks do," Grandpa said.

Cousin Small Duck paddled up,
and he looked at the egg.
"What's that?" he asked Duckling.

"It's our egg, with a baby duck in it,"
Duckling said. "You came in one too."

"I didn't!" said Cousin Small.

"You did!" Duckling said.

"Grandpa says
all ducks do."

"Maybe Grandpa's wrong,"
said Cousin Small.

"Grandpa's *always* right,"
Duckling said. "You just
wait and see."

Mommy Duck sat on the egg.

Daddy Duck came with some food.

"Our egg moved a bit," Duckling told Daddy.

Auntie Duck came with some
feathers to make the nest cozy and nice.
"Our egg jiggled a bit," Duckling told Auntie.

Grandpa Duck came to see
how things were going.

"I heard something inside our egg,"
Duckling told Grandpa.

Mommy Duck stood up.

"It won't be long now," she told Duckling.

All the big ducks were excited.

They stood around the egg, and they quacked.

Quack-quack-quack-quack!

But . . .

nothing happened.

Then Duckling quacked at the egg,
all by himself, very softly.
"Quack-quack-quack!"
and . . .

tap-
tap-
tap!

"Our egg tapped at me!"
Duckling gasped.

Then . . .
crack!
The egg broke.

And out of the shell poked a tiny wee beak,
and a tiny wee head, just like Duckling's,
but very much smaller.

"Oh, my goodness!"
gasped Cousin Small.

It was quacking time
at the lake.

Quack!

Quack!
Quack!

And they all loved
their new baby duck.

The End